W9-ANG-636

To Ryan
from Ester-C
Orchardgate

The Star
who fell out
of the sky

Ian Robson • Ian Newsham

For Charlie and Lucas — all the inspiration a
dad could wish for
I. R.

To my little stars R, E and J
I. N.

First published in 2007 in Great Britain by Gullane Children's Books,
an imprint of Pinwheel Limited, Winchester House, 259-269 Old Marylebone Road, London NW1 5XJ
Text copyright © 2005 by Ian Robson
Illustrations copyright © 2005 by Ian Newsham

This 2007 edition published by Backpack Books by arrangement with Pinwheel Ltd.

All rights reserved. No part of this publication may be reproduced,
stored in a retrieval system, or transmitted in any form or by any means,
electronic, mechanical, photocopying, recording or otherwise, without prior written permission from the publisher.

ISBN -13 : 978-0-7607-9177-6
ISBN-10 : 0-7607-9177-5

Printed and bound in China

1 3 5 7 9 10 8 6 4 2

The Star
who fell out
of the sky

Ian Robson · Ian Newsham

BACK
PACK
BOOKS

It was night and the jungle animals were sitting
around the campfire, looking at the stars.
Suddenly Harold the Hippo saw something unusual.

"Look everybody," he said, "that
star looks like it is falling out of the sky!"
    The animals looked up. There *was* a star falling out of
the sky, heading straight for their fire. The animals
watched as it grew bigger and bigger . . .

They fled into the jungle
just as the star crashed into
the earth beside the fire.

"Ouch!"
said the star.

One by one the animals appeared until they were
all gathered around the star.
"What happened to you?" roared Leonard the Lion.
"I fell out of the sky of course!" said the little star, "and
I really hurt myself when I landed." The star began to cry.
He was very sad. "How can I get back to my friends now?"
he moaned.

"I have an idea . . ." said Harold shyly.

"Don't be silly," scolded Leonard, "you never have good ideas.
I will have to have an idea." All the animals turned to Leonard.
"I am the strongest animal in the jungle," he boasted, "so I will
pick up the star and throw it as hard as I can back into the sky."

The little star looked
worried by this idea but he
agreed to do as Leonard said.
The lion picked up the star . . .

and threw him as hard as
he could up into the sky.

The star got smaller and smaller as it flew higher and higher into the sky.

Soon it was almost the same size as all the other stars.

"There," said Leonard looking very pleased with himself. "I have sent the little star back to his friends."

But, as the animals watched,
the star began to get bigger . . .
and bigger. It was falling back
towards the jungle.
The animals ran for cover.

Once again the little star landed with a heavy thump.
"Ouch, that *really* hurt!" he said.
"I'm sorry," said Leonard. "I did my best. Now I
don't know *how* we can get you back up into the sky."

"I know," said
Harold the Hippo very shyly.
"I know — I have an idea."

"Don't be silly — you never have any
good ideas," said Edward the Elephant crossly. "*I* have an idea."
All the animals looked at Edward. "I'll put the star on the
end of my trunk, blow as hard as I can, and the star
will shoot up into the sky."

For the second time the star looked worried. But once more he agreed to the plan. Edward picked him up, put him on the end of his trunk . . .

and blew out a great big breath of air.

The star rose up into the sky,
getting smaller and smaller
until it was almost the same
size as the other stars.

The star stopped for a
moment and Edward looked
very pleased. "There you
are," he said. "I've done it!"

"Uh-oh!" said Milly Monkey as the star began to fall back towards the campfire. "No you haven't."

The star landed hard beside the animals. "Ouch and ouch again," said the star, "this is getting silly."

This time, before Harold could say a word, Percy and
Pandora the parrots squawked together. "We have an idea.
We can lift up the little star and fly him back up to his friends."

Still the little star looked worried, but once more
he agreed to the idea. The parrots picked up the star
and flew off into the sky. They flew higher and higher
and higher until they were almost out of sight.

Just as the animals thought that the parrots had returned the star to his friends, they heard a loud squawk from above and soon after Percy and Pandora landed in a heap beside the fire, closely followed by the little star.

"Owww — that really, really hurt," shouted the little star.
"Does no one have an idea that will work?"

For a little while, nobody said a word.

Eventually, in a very quiet voice, Harold said, "*I do*."
The animals all looked at Harold. "We'll build a rocket
to take the little star back to his friends. Everyone
knows that rockets are the best way to get to the stars!"

The animals said nothing until finally Leonard spoke. "That, Harold, is an *excellent* idea!"

For the next two days
the animals worked on the
rocket until it was ready.

They became great friends with the little star who told them all about the other stars and how beautiful the earth looked from space. When it was time for Harold to take the little star back, the animals were very sad.

Just before the little star and Harold climbed into the rocket, Percy and Pandora gave them special helmets they'd made from coconut shells.

And Milly Monkey gave them a bunch of bananas to eat on their trip.

Then, Harold, who was very proud of his idea, climbed into the rocket to take the little star home.

The rocket
took off and
rose slowly
into the sky.

After a while it began to speed up
and soon it was racing into space!
The other animals watched until the
rocket had disappeared from view.

That night, Harold returned. The animals were really pleased to see him.

"Well done, Harold!" they chanted.

"I couldn't have done it without all of you!" replied Harold, very shyly.

And as they all gazed up into the darkness . . .

there in the sky they saw
the little star, twinkling
happily beside his friends!